A HALLOWEEN
MASK FOR MONSTER

Virginia Mueller
pictures by Lynn Munsinger

Puffin Books

PUFFIN BOOKS
Published by the Penguin Group
Penguin Books USA Inc., 375 Hudson Street, New York, New York 10014, U.S.A.
Penguin Books Ltd, 27 Wrights Lane, London W8 5TZ, England
Penguin Books Australia Ltd, Ringwood, Victoria, Australia
Penguin Books Canada Ltd, 10 Alcorn Avenue, Toronto, Ontario, Canada M4V 3B2
Penguin Books (N.Z.) Ltd, 182–190 Wairau Road, Auckland 10, New Zealand

Penguin Books Ltd, Registered Offices: Harmondsworth, Middlesex, England

First published in the United States of America by Albert Whitman & Company, 1986
Published in Picture Puffins 1988
5   7   9   10   8   6
Text copyright © Virginia Mueller, 1986
Illustrations copyright © Lynn Munsinger, 1986
All rights reserved
Printed in Hong Kong
Set in Helvetica

Library of Congress Cataloging in Publication Data
Mueller, Virginia.
A Halloween mask for Monster/Virginia Mueller; pictures by Lynn Munsinger
p. cm.—(Picture puffins)
Summary: Monster tries on girl, boy, cat, and dog masks at
Halloween but since they are all too scary he decides to go as himself.
ISBN 0-14-050879-1
[1. Halloween—Fiction.   2. Monsters—Fiction.]   I. Munsinger,
Lynn. ill.   II. Title. [PZ7.M879Hal 1988]   [E]—dc19   88-11707

To Donna Pape, my mentor. *V.M.*

To Sarah. *L.M.*

It was Halloween.

Monster tried on a girl mask.

"Too scary," Monster said.

Monster tried on a boy mask.

"Too scary," Monster said.

Monster tried on a dog mask.

"Too scary," Monster said.

Monster tried on a cat mask.

"Too scary," Monster said.

Monster looked in the mirror.

He saw his own face.

"Just right," Monster said.